Dear Brother

Also by
Alison McGhee

Dear Sister

What I Leave Behind

Pablo and Birdy

Maybe a Fox
(with Kathi Appelt)

Firefly Hollow

Someday

Making a Friend

So Many Days

Little Boy

Star Bright

Dear Brother

a graphic novel-ish by
Alison McGhee

illustrated by
Tuan Nini

A Caitlyn Dlouhy Book

Atheneum Books for Young Readers
atheneum   New York   London   Toronto   Sydney   New Delhi

atheneum

ATHENEUM BOOKS FOR YOUNG READERS
An imprint of Simon & Schuster Children's Publishing Division
1230 Avenue of the Americas, New York, New York 10020

ATHENEUM BOOKS FOR YOUNG READERS is a
registered trademark of Simon & Schuster, Inc.
Atheneum logo is a trademark of Simon & Schuster, Inc.

For information about special discounts for bulk purchases,
please contact Simon & Schuster Special Sales at 1-866-506-1949
or business@simonandschuster.com.

The Simon & Schuster Speakers Bureau can bring authors to your
live event. For more information or to book an event, contact the
Simon & Schuster Speakers Bureau at 1-866-248-3049 or
visit our website at www.simonspeakers.com.

Interior design by Rebecca Syracuse
The text for this book was hand-lettered.
The illustrations for this book were rendered in mixed media.
Manufactured in China
0423 SCP
First Edition
2 4 6 8 10 9 7 5 3 1
CIP data for this book is available from the Library of Congress.
ISBN 9781534487086
ISBN 9781534487109 (ebook)

For beautiful Cleo. And to Devon and Matt,
the humans who loved and cared for her.
— A. M.

To Abang and Kakak, there is no home without you.
To Şerban and Ooshi, for life, oh beautiful life.
—T. N.

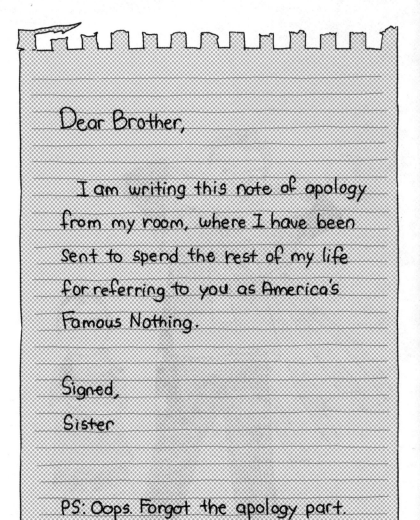

Dear Brother,

I am writing this note of apology from my room, where I have been sent to spend the rest of my life for referring to you as America's Famous Nothing.

Signed,
Sister

PS: Oops. Forgot the apology part.

Dear Brother,

   I apologize for calling you
America's Famous Nothing.

Signed,
Sister

PS: Even if it's true.

PPS: In my defense, I'm tired of
     you proclaiming yourself
     America's Famous Everything.

For evidence, I present to you…

our family photo album!

AMERICA'S FAMOUS MAGICIAN

<u>Exhibit A:</u>
Watch as America's Famous Magician saws his trusty sidekick in half and puts her back together!

Oops.

<u>Exhibit B:</u>
America's Famous Magician attempts the apple-on-the-head trick with his trusty sidekick!

Oops.

Exhibit C: America's Famous Magician makes his trusty sidekick *disappear!*

Oops.

Double Oops.

Triple Oops.

This is what it's like to be me, America's Overlooked Sibling. I mean, just how long was I missing?

AMERICA'S FAMOUS DAREDEVIL

Exhibit A:
America's Famous Daredevil and his trusty sidekick attempt to scale impossible heights!

Oops.

Exhibit B:
America's Famous Daredevil and his trusty sidekick sled down a never-before-attempted hill!

Oops.

*Note: Viewer discretion is advised for the following series of photographs:

America's Famous Daredevil and his trusty sidekick leap a never-before-attempted Double Boardslide down the front steps!

AMERICA'S FAMOUS KID CHEF

<u>Exhibit A</u>: America's Famous Kid Chef and his trusty sidekick prepare the ingredients for his Thousand-Ingredient Chopped Salad.

<u>Exhibit B</u>: America's Famous Kid Chef and his trusty sidekick prepare the ingredients for his Famous Thousand-Layer Dip.

Exhibit C:
Trusty sidekick
cleans up after
America's
Famous Kid
Chef.

I had to call in the reinforcements for that one.

Thank you, Jorinda. Thank you, Kareem.

And finally, we come to the latest in the America's Famous Nothing series.

AMERICA'S FAMOUS BANJO BROTHERS

<u>Exhibit A</u>: In which America's Famous Banjo Brothers and their trusty sidekick set up for their first-ever show!

Exhibit B: In which America's Famous Banjo Brothers perform for the public!

Exhibit C: In which America's Famous Banjo Brothers plan their first-ever North American tour!

Notice anything similar
about these photos?

Me too.

SOMEONE is in the background
of every single one.

Someone who gets no recognition.

Someone who does all the work while America's Famous Nothing gets all the attention.

Gee, who could that someone be?

Welcome to my world!

POP QUIZ!

A. Does anyone in this family ever notice how much the younger sibling wants a dog? Y/N

B. Does anyone ever notice how good the younger sibling is at playing the bongo drums? **Y/N**

C. Does anyone think to ask her if she ever gets tired of always being overlooked? **Y/N**

D. Does anyone notice her **AT ALL?**
Y/N

It wasn't always this way.

See this photo?

And this one?

And this one?

And this one?

Before the whole America's Famous thing, he was just...my brother.

Here I am, playing my latest original song for bongo drums and solo vocalist, *"He Ain't Famous, He's My Brother,"* to a crowd of adoring fans.

Thank you, dogs, for always noticing me, always listening to my original songs for bongo drums and solo vocalist, and always being my adoring fans.

You're the only ones.

Today we present the latest episode of...

TODAY'S INJUSTICE

in which it is announced that Brother gets to go to music camp, even though **I** like music too, and **I**'m good at music too, and why is it always the **YOUNGER** sibling who has to wait their turn, because that is **NOT FAIR**.

Once again, Brother gets exactly what he wants, while Sister gets...

Who got to choose the chores
he wanted?

"you'll get your turn when you're older."

Who got to choose where we went
for our family vacation?

"Sorry, honey, we're out of time."

Nothing around here ever changes.

BUT IT'S ABOUT TO!

**SOMEONE** in this family
is older now.

SOMEONE'S turn is
/oooo O O O O O o ooong
<u>overdue.</u>

And now that it's time
to choose a family pet,
SOMEONE in this house
is about to get their turn!

Someone in this family has always wanted a dog, while someone ELSE in this family wants a... *bearded dragon.*

I think we can all agree there's only one real choice here.

SORRY, HONEY, DOGS AREN'T ALLOWED IN OUR APARTMENT BUILDING. WE THOUGHT YOU KNEW THAT.

WE DON'T MAKE THE RULES.

BUT GOOD NEWS! GUESS WHAT **ARE** ALLOWED? BEARDED DRAGONS!

YAY! A BEARDED DRAGON IT IS!!

BEARDED DRAGONS ARE ...

Dear everyone in our apartment building,

I apologize for waking up the babies in 4B and 7C. I apologize for waking up Mr. Rodriguez in 3D, who works late on the third shift.

I also apologize to everyone who thought someone in 5A was being murdered.

Sincerely,
Someone in 5A

PS: In my defense, a part of me **WAS** being murdered. The part that has always wanted a dog.

DIDN'T KNOW I WANTED A DOG SO MUCH?!
I'VE ONLY WANTED A DOG MY WHOLE ENTIRE LIFE!
DON'T YOU PEOPLE EVEN KNOW WHO I AM??!!

I hereby vow to remain silent until this family finally notices me!

Not only **NOTICES** me, but sees that I'm already good at things!

Like playing the bongo drums!

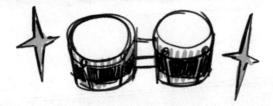

The day will soon come when
Brother will **BEG ME**
to join his banjo band.

Here I am eating breakfast
and not saying a word.

Here I am doing my chores
and not saying a word.

Here I am listening to Brother and our parents discussing all the zillions of things we need to get for our future ~~non dog pet that I never wanted in the first place~~ bearded dragon and not saying a word.

Here I am, playing my latest original composition for bongo drums and solo vocalist, "*The Sound of Silence*," on my bongo drums and not singing a word (very loudly).

Dear Brother,

I am writing this note of apology for ~~yelling~~ ~~shouting~~ screaming at you after I calmly informed you that no one even noticed I hadn't said a single word for an entire day and you said, "Ohhhh! **THAT'S** why it was the best day of my life."

Signed,
Sister

PS: Oops. Forgot the apology part.

Dear Brother,

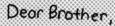

SORRY.
(not)

Signed,

Sister

PS: I don't get why you thought
you were being funny.

PPS: It's **NOT** funny.

Dear Brother,

I have a question.

Why don't **YOU** ever have to write **ME** a note of apology?

Let me show you how it's done.

Dear Sister,

I am sorry that no one in this family ever stops to think about how YOU feel.

I am sorry that everyone in this family thinks about ME, America's Famous Nothing, instead of you.

I am also sorry that I get to have everything I have ever wanted, like music camp and a bearded dragon, while you don't get anything.

Why am I sorry? Because you are the <u>greatest sister</u> in the history of the world, and I am **very** lucky that you were born.

With eternal love and devotion,
Brother

Dear Brother,

Even though the note of apology on the previous page was fake, and I wrote it myself, I accept your apology.

That is because someone in this apartment is a better person than you.

Signed,
Someone in this apartment

Dear Brother,

Someday, when I'm older,
maybe I'll write the note of apology
I was sent to this room to write.

Someday, when I'm older,
maybe I won't mind that
life is so unfair.

Someday, when I'm older,
maybe I'll stop wishing you
were a dog instead of a boy.

However, that day
has not yet come.

Signed,
Sister

Time to call in
the reinforcements.

Maybe not.

It's me and you, dogs.

Stuck here until we're older.

Much, much older.

Dear Brother,
    Here is a story I wrote.
I hope you enjoy it.

Crushed Dreams

Once upon a time there was a little
sister who loved dogs. But her building
didn't allow them.

Then, even though the little sister had never wanted a bearded dragon, her big brother and her parents decided to get one.

All the sister's dreams were crushed and she was never happy again.

The End.

Dear Brother,
   Here is another story I wrote.
I hope you enjoy it.

Eternal Sorrow

Once upon a time there was a girl.
She had wanted a dog her entire life.

Then, for reasons beyond her control,
she found herself forced to live
with a bearded dragon.

The girl lived in eternal sorrow
for the rest of her life.

The End.

Dear future person reading this,

Let it be known that long, long ago, there was a girl whose dreams were crushed and she lived in sorrow for the rest of her life.

Signed,
A girl who lived a long, long time ago

Dear Brother,

Yes. I know today's the day. Pretty sure **EVERYONE** knows today's the day.

Signed,
Sister

PS: Just out of curiosity, were you as
excited for me to be born as you are
for this ~~non-dog pet I never wanted~~
~~in the first place~~ creature to arrive?

Don't answer that.

PPS: Also just out of curiosity, did
anyone write an original banjo
composition for me when **I** arrived?

Pretty sure we all know the
answer to that one too.

THEY KICKED YOU OUT
OF THE APARTMENT?

Dear future person reading this,

Do they have bearded dragons in the future?

If not, allow me to introduce you to one.

Are you ready?
Please turn the page.

Take a look at these covert photos, captured by an unknown wildlife photographer.

This is me trying to do my homework while it stares at me.

This is me trying to read a book while it stares at me.

This is me playing cards with Jorinda and Kareem while it stares at us.

This is me playing my bongo drums while it stares at me.

POP QUIZ

What did all those photos have in common?

A. A non-dog pet that someone in this family never wanted in the first place.

B. A non-dog pet that someone in this family never wanted in the first place, never taking its eyes off her.

C. The words "while it stares at me."

D. All of the above.

~~To Whom It May Concern~~

~~To the Bearded Creature This May Concern~~

~~To a Certain Creature That Now Lives
in This Apartment Against Someone's Will~~

To You Know Who You Are,

On a scale of one to ten, how much
do you enjoy staring at me?

1
2
3
4
5
6
7
8
9
10

11

I KNEW IT.

Dear Brother,

Yes, I know she's supposed to be **OUR** pet, even though only <u>one of us</u> wanted a bearded dragon.

Yes, I know I'm supposed to pay attention to her too, even though only <u>one of us</u> wanted a bearded dragon.

Maybe someday,

WHEN I'M **OLDER**,

I'll consider it.

Signed,
Sister

According to a random survey of this household, which animal member has been voted Most Unpopular?

Please circle only one answer.

A. Bearded dragon

B. Bearded dragon

C. Bearded dragon

D. Bearded dragon

Dear Brother,

I am sorry you did not like the name I suggested for ~~your~~ our pet.

Signed,
Sister

PS: I can't help it if I think
Frightful is a good one.

Dear Brother,

You know how much
you love Frightful?

That's how much I would
have loved the dog I
wasn't allowed to get.

Signed,
Sister

Look at these photos of Jorinda's
big brother and her...

and Kareem's big brother and him.

And now take a look at this one of **MY** big brother and me!

Kidding.

Dear Brother,

Someday they will make a T-shirt in honor of me. The T-shirt will say:

Spoiler alert: The T-shirt will be a huge hit worldwide. All the overlooked younger siblings will walk around wearing their T-shirts, and whenever we see each other, we will cry in solidarity.

Consider yourself warned.

Signed,
Sister

Dear Brother,

Please enjoy this photo of the costume I got for your ~~one true love~~ Frightful.

Now she'll be all set for trick-or-treating next Halloween.

WHAT?
It's so cute!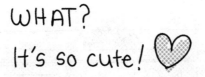

Signed,
Sister

Dear Brother,

Please enjoy this photo of the cute sweater I found for Frightful.

Shot down
again.

Signed,
Sister

Dear future person reading this,

Do they still have crickets in the future?

If not, here is a fun fact about crickets: No matter where you keep them, you can still hear them.

Don't ask how I know this.

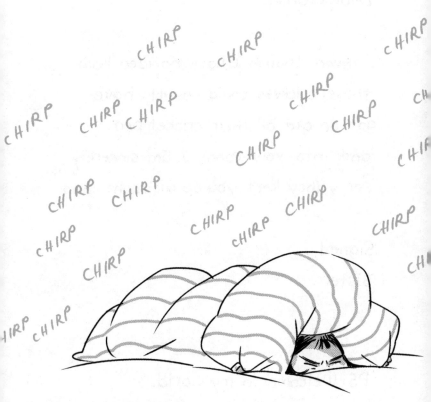

Signed,
Tired of chirping

Dear Brother,

    Even though I have no idea how
those crickets could possibly have
gotten out of their cricket pen
and into your room, I am sincerely
sorry they kept you up all night long.

Signed,
Sister

PS: Welcome to my world.

Dear crickets,

Did you enjoy your freedom?

Did you make the most of it?

Did it feel good to hop and jump and sing and sing and sing all night long?

Are you grateful to the unknown someone who let you out of your prison?

Good. Because no one else is.

Signed,
Unknown someone

S.O.S.!

Gentledogs of the jury,

Thank you for coming to my emergency meeting. We have a dire situation on our hands. See this brochure of Brother's music camp?

This is where Brother and his banjo will be spending **AN ENTIRE MONTH.** Which we already knew.

But what we did **NOT** know is
that someone in this apartment
will be in charge of a certain non-dog
creature while Brother is gone.

For the **ENTIRE MONTH**.

Because guess what?
Bearded dragons aren't
allowed at music camp.

Dear Brother,

I apologize for ~~screaming~~ ~~yelling~~ calmly informing you that it is **100%**
UNFAIR that the <u>one</u> person in this family who **NEVER WANTED** a bearded dragon in the first place has to take care of ~~your one true love~~ Frightful while you're away at music camp.

Signed,
Sister

PS: Also, if you are so afraid to leave ~~your one true love~~ Frightful with me, you should have thought of that before you signed up for music camp.

Here are some photos I took of Brother and his one true love last night.

NO, I was **NOT** snooping.

I mean, haven't **YOU** ever had to pee in the middle of the night?

But sometimes when you're not snooping you still hear things you're not supposed to hear.

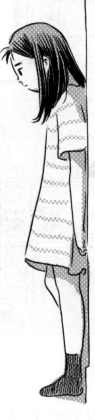

Like how nervous someone is to be going to music camp by himself.

How he wishes Darius and Theo
were coming with him.

How he doesn't want to
leave his ~~one true love~~
bearded dragon.

You know what? If I had to go to music camp with just my bongo drums for one whole month, without Jorinda, without Kareem, and without the dog I would have loved the way someone loves his bearded dragon, I might be nervous too.

Might.

PS: You want to know
what's weird?

I didn't think America's
Famous Nothing ever got
nervous about anything.

Dear Brother,

This is not a note of apology and no one told me to write it.

I hope you have fun at music camp.

Signed,
Sister

PS: I mean it.

PPS: Also, don't worry about your ~~one true love~~ bearded dragon.

PPPS: I don't get why she has to stay in my room, but WHATEVER.

02:23pm
Red peppers: ✓
Fresh water: ✓
Clean incubator: ✓
Crickets: UGH. ✓
Light bulb: ✓
Affection:
02:23pm
It's going to be a long, long month.
Signed,
Sister
02:23pm

Dear future person reading this,

Do they have bad dreams
in the future?

If not, this is a photo, taken
in the middle of the night, of
the kind of thing that caused
bad dreams for people who
lived a long time ago.

Signed,
A girl who lived a long,
long time ago

Red peppers: ✓
Fresh water: ✓
Clean incubator: ✓
Crickets: UGH. ✓
Light bulb: ✓
Affection: 😱
Signed,
Sister
10:12am
PS: Aren't you sick of camp by now? Can't you come home?
10:13am

Dear Brother,
Jorinda and Kareem and I are having a sleepover. Don't worry. ~~Your one true love~~ Frightful is also present.

10:14 pm

Is it fun, you ask? Yes. But guess what? It's not as fun as I thought it would be.

Signed,
Sister

10:14 pm

10:15 pm

Don't get used to all that attention, Frightful. Because tomorrow things go back to normal around here.

Normal?

"BUT WE DON'T WANT
HER TO BE LONELY!"

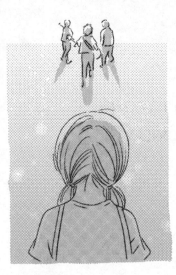

Frightful,
do I
ignore you?

Do you wish I paid
more attention
to you?

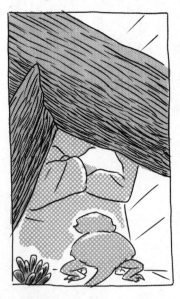

Huh.

Dear future person reading this,

Do friends still exist in the future?

If so, do your friends sometimes annoy you?

But also sometimes... make you think?

Just wondering.

Signed,
A girl who lived a long, long time ago

Gentledogs of the jury,

I have gathered you here today to discuss the health and wellbeing of the non-dog in our midst.

Does the non-dog in our midst look like she would enjoy dressing up a little?

All in favor,
say aye.

All opposed,
say nay.

The ayes have it!

Please take a look at these photos of a brand-new line of accessories created especially for bearded dragons and approved by a jury of gentledogs.

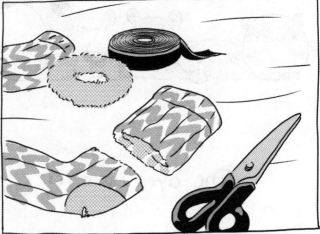

Please take a look at these photos of America's Famous Bearded Dragon modeling the accessories.

Dear future person reading this,

Please take a look at this photo from long ago, of America's Famous Bearded Dragon and someone in this apartment who is being forced to take care of her all month.

Don't tell anyone, but...
I'm almost enjoying this.

Signed,
A girl who lived a long,
   long time ago

PS: Don't get excited now.
I said <u>almost</u>.

Well, well, well,
what do we have here?

Who knew that bearded dragons loved music so much?

Who knew that America's overlooked sibling was capable of starting her **OWN** band?

Here is a possible title
for the book of my life.

Frightful, please take a look of America's Famous Banjo Brother photos from music camp.

Hmm.

Let's compare these photos to the other America's Famous photos.

Do we sense a disturbance in the Force?

10:13 pm
Sister
How is Frightful's appetite, is she eating okay?
9:52pm
Dear Brother,
To answer your questions,
Frightful is doing GREAT.
In fact, Frightful is thriving.
10:09pm
That's because America's Famous Sister is taking incredible care of her.
Signed,
Sister
10:10pm
PS: I'm sorry you're not having as

Dear future person reading this,

Do brothers and sisters still exist
in the future?

If so, does the idea of your
brother finally being the overlooked
one make you kind of...sad?

Just wondering.

Signed,
A girl who lived a long,
long time ago

Dear Brother,
Here are more photos of ~~your one true love Frightful~~ OUR FAVORITE BEARDED DRAGON.
5:25pm

+6
5:26pm

Frightful wants you to know that even though America's Famous Sister is taking ~~great wonderful~~ perfect care of her, she misses you.

Signed,
Sister
5:28pm

PS: Also, ~~your one true love Frightful~~ OUR FAVORITE DRAGON wants you to know that she thinks you're good at playing the banjo.
5:29pm

PPS: So do I. Kind of.
5:31pm

Even if I don't like to tell him
that because, you know, the whole
America's Famous thing.

THESE are the music camp talent show winners?

The Saxophone Sisters

The Erhu Extraordinaires

The Brilliant
Bagpipes

The Magnificent Marimbas

Frightful,
are you thinking
the same thing
I'm thinking?

I mean, even if he's not the
best player at music camp,
he **IS** good at playing the banjo.

Pretty good, anyway.

Even if he does drive us
kind of bananas.

Even if he's not as good at
playing the banjo as we are
at playing the bongos.

Right?

Dear Brother,

I do not have any photos to share with you today. Which is a good thing. By the time you read this, today will be a memory. Which is also a good thing, because it was the worst day of my life.

Today was the day that Frightful almost died.

Don't worry! Remember, I said ALMOST! And by the time you read this it will be in the distant, distant past.

It's a long story. So I'm just going to give you some key words and you can fill in the blanks.

DEAD??

FRIGHTFUUUL!!!!

MOUTH-TO-MOUTH
RESUSCITATION??

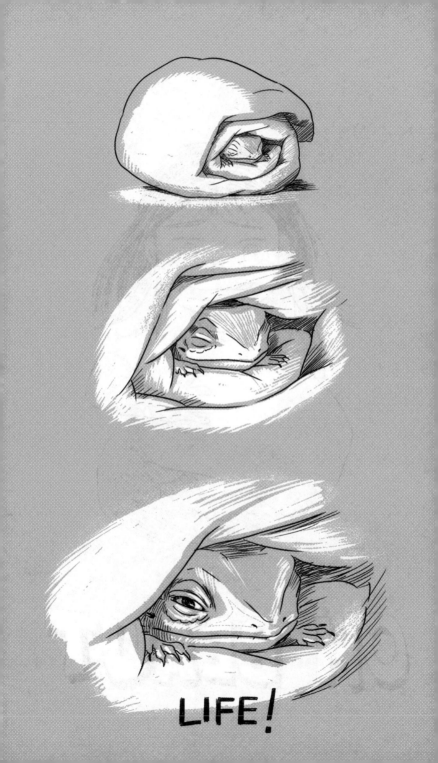

LIFE!

Dear Brother,

Thank you for your letter. I agree.
Some things are too important for
texting.

I say it was the day
Frightful almost died.

You say it was the day
I saved Frightful's life.

~~Signed,~~
~~Sincerely,~~
~~Best regards,~~
~~With affection,~~
~~Warmly,~~
♥
Sister

Sooooooo, I've been looking through the old family photo album again.

Here's a photo from that birthday when I was sick and had to cancel my party.

And America's Famous Magician performed a one-person magic show.

Here's another from the time when America's Famous Daredevil rescued his sister from a deadly wild animal.

Here's another from the time when America's Famous Kid Chef prepared a special treat for his sous-chef.

Hmm.

Dear future person reading this,
and gentledogs of the jury,
Let the record show that my
brother was not entirely bad.

Signed,
A girl who lived a long,
long time ago

Gentledogs of the jury,

Thank you for your faithful service.

As pertains to the case of
Brother vs. Sister, let the record
show that Sister has decided to
drop the case.

For the time being,
anyway.

Dear Brother,

In a few days you'll be home!

Someone in this apartment
can't wait to see you!

That someone even got a new
outfit just for the occasion!

Sister

PS: Someone else in this apartment
   is also not entirely sad at the
   thought of seeing you.

PPS: For real.

Please take a look at these photos
of Brother's welcome home party.

The sign!

The cake!

The original song composed and performed by America's Famous Bongo Band and America's Famous Bearded Dragon!

Dear future person reading this,

Guess what? Sometimes, when you're older, your turn actually comes.

For evidence, I enclose this photo of America's Famous Bearded Bongo Banjo Band.

Signed,
A girl who lived a long, long time ago

PS: Do you even have photos in the future?

WELCOME TO MY NEW PHOTO ALBUM.
Want to take a look?

The Bearded Bongo Banjo Band's FIRST SHOW!

The Bearded Bongo Banjo Band GOES ON TOUR!

The Bearded Bongo Banjo Band Tours Some More!

The Bearded Bongo Banjo Band Graciously Accepts Award

The Bearded Bongo Banjo Bandmates Relax At Home Surrounded by Their Adoring Fans.

Brother was right.

Living a life of fame is great.

But you know what's <u>greater</u>?

Alison McGhee is the *New York Times* bestselling author of *Someday*, as well as *Dear Sister*, *What I Leave Behind*, *Maybe a Fox* with Kathi Appelt, *Firefly Hollow*, and *Little Boy*, to name a few. She divides her time between Minneapolis, Minnesota, and Laguna Beach, California. You can visit her at AlisonMcGhee.com.

Nini Farhana Tuan (she goes by Nini) grew up in Subang Jaya, Malaysia, and received her fine arts degree from the National University of Fine Arts in Bucharest, Romania. She makes illustrations, comics, and animation, and this is her book debut. She now resides in Bucharest, and you can visit her at Tuannini.com.